MOBY TRUMP

A NAKED BOOK*

COPYRIGHT © 2017

ISBN: 9781973479031

MOBY TRUMP

"My cake is dough."
— **William Shakespeare**

"In Xanadu did Kubla Khan
A stately pleasure-dome decree:
Where Alph, the sacred river, ran
Through caverns measureless to man
Down to a sunless sea."
S.T. Coleridge

This Page Intentionally left blank.

This Page Intentionally left blank.

This Page Intentionally left blank.

This Page Intentionally left blank.

This Page Intentionally left blank.

This Page Intentionally left blank.

This Page Intentionally left blank.

This Page Intentionally left blank.

This Page Intentionally left blank.

This Page Intentionally left blank.

This Page Intentionally left blank.

This Page Intentionally left blank.

This Page Intentionally left blank.

This Page Intentionally left blank.

This Page Intentionally left blank.

This Page Intentionally left blank.

This Page Intentionally left blank.

This Page Intentionally left blank.

This Page Intentionally left blank.

This Page Intentionally left blank.

This Page Intentionally left blank.

This Page Intentionally left blank.

This Page Intentionally left blank.

This Page Intentionally left blank.

This Page Intentionally left blank.

This Page Intentionally left blank.

This Page Intentionally left blank.

This Page Intentionally left blank.

This Page Intentionally left blank.

This Page Intentionally left blank.

This Page Intentionally left blank.

This Page Intentionally left blank.

This Page Intentionally left blank.

This Page Intentionally left blank.

This Page Intentionally left blank.

This Page Intentionally left blank.

This Page Intentionally left blank.

This Page Intentionally left blank.

This Page Intentionally left blank.

This Page Intentionally left blank.

This Page Intentionally left blank.

This Page Intentionally left blank.

This Page Intentionally left blank.

This Page Intentionally left blank.

This Page Intentionally left blank.

This Page Intentionally left blank.

This Page Intentionally left blank.

This Page Intentionally left blank.

This Page Intentionally left blank.

This Page Intentionally left blank.

This Page Intentionally left blank.

This Page Intentionally left blank.

This Page Intentionally left blank.

This Page Intentionally left blank.

This Page Intentionally left blank.

This Page Intentionally left blank.

This Page Intentionally left blank.

This Page Intentionally left blank.

This Page Intentionally left blank.

This Page Intentionally left blank.

This Page Intentionally left blank.

This Page Intentionally left blank.

This Page Intentionally left blank.

This Page Intentionally left blank.

This Page Intentionally left blank.

This Page Intentionally left blank.

This Page Intentionally left blank.

This Page Intentionally left blank.

This Page Intentionally left blank.

This Page Intentionally left blank.

This Page Intentionally left blank.

This Page Intentionally left blank.

This Page Intentionally left blank.

This Page Intentionally left blank.

This Page Intentionally left blank.

This Page Intentionally left blank.

This Page Intentionally left blank.

This Page Intentionally left blank.

This Page Intentionally left blank.

This Page Intentionally left blank.

This Page Intentionally left blank.

This Page Intentionally left blank.

This Page Intentionally left blank.

This Page Intentionally left blank.

This Page Intentionally left blank.

This Page Intentionally left blank.

This Page Intentionally left blank.

This Page Intentionally left blank.

This Page Intentionally left blank.

This Page Intentionally left blank.

This Page Intentionally left blank.

This Page Intentionally left blank.

This Page Intentionally left blank.

This Page Intentionally left blank.

This Page Intentionally left blank.

This Page Intentionally left blank.

This Page Intentionally left blank.

This Page Intentionally left blank.

This Page Intentionally left blank.

This Page Intentionally left blank.

This Page Intentionally left blank.

This Page Intentionally left blank.

This Page Intentionally left blank.

This Page Intentionally left blank.

This Page Intentionally left blank.

This Page Intentionally left blank.

This Page Intentionally left blank.

This Page Intentionally left blank.

This Page Intentionally left blank.

This Page Intentionally left blank.

This Page Intentionally left blank.

This Page Intentionally left blank.

This Page Intentionally left blank.

This Page Intentionally left blank.

This Page Intentionally left blank.

This Page Intentionally left blank.

This Page Intentionally left blank.

This Page Intentionally left blank.

This Page Intentionally left blank.

This Page Intentionally left blank.

This Page Intentionally left blank.

This Page Intentionally left blank.

This Page Intentionally left blank.

This Page Intentionally left blank.

This Page Intentionally left blank.

This Page Intentionally left blank.

This Page Intentionally left blank.

This Page Intentionally left blank.

This Page Intentionally left blank.

This Page Intentionally left blank.

This Page Intentionally left blank.

This Page Intentionally left blank.

This Page Intentionally left blank.

This Page Intentionally left blank.

This Page Intentionally left blank.

This Page Intentionally left blank.

This Page Intentionally left blank.

This Page Intentionally left blank.

This Page Intentionally left blank.

This Page Intentionally left blank.

This Page Intentionally left blank.

This Page Intentionally left blank.

This Page Intentionally left blank.

This Page Intentionally left blank.

This Page Intentionally left blank.

This Page Intentionally left blank.

This Page Intentionally left blank.

This Page Intentionally left blank.

This Page Intentionally left blank.

This Page Intentionally left blank.

This Page Intentionally left blank.

This Page Intentionally left blank.

This Page Intentionally left blank.

This Page Intentionally left blank.

This Page Intentionally left blank.

This Page Intentionally left blank.

This Page Intentionally left blank.

This Page Intentionally left blank.

This Page Intentionally left blank.

This Page Intentionally left blank.

This Page Intentionally left blank.

This Page Intentionally left blank.

This Page Intentionally left blank.

This Page Intentionally left blank.

This Page Intentionally left blank.

This Page Intentionally left blank.

This Page Intentionally left blank.

This Page Intentionally left blank.

This Page Intentionally left blank.

This Page Intentionally left blank.

This Page Intentionally left blank.

This Page Intentionally left blank.

This Page Intentionally left blank.

This Page Intentionally left blank.

This Page Intentionally left blank.

This Page Intentionally left blank.

This Page Intentionally left blank.

This Page Intentionally left blank.

This Page Intentionally left blank.

This Page Intentionally left blank.

This Page Intentionally left blank.

This Page Intentionally left blank.

This Page Intentionally left blank.

This Page Intentionally left blank.

This Page Intentionally left blank.

This Page Intentionally left blank.

This Page Intentionally left blank.

This Page Intentionally left blank.

This Page Intentionally left blank.

This Page Intentionally left blank.

This Page Intentionally left blank.

This Page Intentionally left blank.

This Page Intentionally left blank.

This Page Intentionally left blank.

This Page Intentionally left blank.

This Page Intentionally left blank.

This Page Intentionally left blank.

This Page Intentionally left blank.

This Page Intentionally left blank.

This Page Intentionally left blank.

This Page Intentionally left blank.

This Page Intentionally left blank.

This Page Intentionally left blank.

This Page Intentionally left blank.

The End!

Made in the USA
Middletown, DE
12 December 2017